Friends Are Like That!

Friends Are Like That!

Stories to Read to Yourself

SELECTED BY THE
Child Study Children's Book
Committee at Bank Street

Illustrated by Leigh Grant

THOMAS Y. CROWELL • NEW YORK

Library of Congress Cataloging in Publication Data
Main entry under title:
Friends are like that!
SUMMARY: Selections by 10 authors including
Charlotte Zolotow, Eloise Greenfield, and Astrid Lindgren
depict the many facets of friendship.
1. Children's stories, American. [1. Friendship—Fiction.
2. Short stories] I. Grant, Leigh.
II. Child Study Children's Book Committee at Bank Street.
PZ5.F917 [Fic] 78-22513
ISBN 0-690-03979-4 ISBN 0-690-03980-8 lib. bdg.

10 9 8 7 6 5 4 3 2 1
First Edition

This book is dedicated
to the children, teachers, and staff
of Bank Street College of Education.

Contents

Acknowledgments

The publishers gratefully acknowledge permission to reprint the following:

"Why I Like Charlie" by James Flora, excerpted and reprinted by permission of Harcourt Brace Jovanovich, Inc., from *My Friend Charlie*, copyright © 1964 by James Flora.

"Janey" by Charlotte Zolotow, reprinted by permission of Harper & Row, Publishers, Inc., from *Janey*, text copyright © 1973 by Charlotte Zolotow.

"Stevie" by John Steptoe, reprinted by permission of Harper & Row, Publishers, Inc., from *Stevie*, copyright © 1969 by John L. Steptoe.

"Boys Just Can't Keep a Secret" by Astrid Lindgren, reprinted by permission of the author and The Viking Press, Inc., from *Happy Times in Noisy Village*, copyright © 1961 by Astrid Lindgren and copyright © 1963 by The Viking Press, Inc.

"The Children's Theater" by Carolyn Haywood, reprinted by permission of William Morrow & Company, Inc., from *Annie Pat and Eddie*, copyright © 1960 by Carolyn Haywood.

"Two and Me Makes Three" by Roberta Greene, adapted by permission of Coward, McCann and Geoghegan, Inc., from *Two and Me Makes Three*, copyright © 1970 by Roberta Greene.

"Me and Neesie" by Eloise Greenfield, reprinted by permission of

The Committee acknowledges with deep appreciation the skilled and
dedicated work of Bernice (Bunny) Greenwald, who shepherded this
anthology from its inception to its publication.

Friends Are Like That!

Why I Like Charlie

BY JAMES FLORA

My friend Charlie is a pretty good old friend. I couldn't like him any better than I do, even if he owned a pony and an air rifle.

There are lots of reasons why I like Charlie.

Here are some:

1. He gives me half of whatever he is eating.
2. Sometimes he lets me be the pitcher in the ball game, even though he owns the ball.

3. Charlie never laughs at my nose.
4. Sometimes when I am about to be eaten by dragons, Charlie saves me.
5. Once when I cut my hand, Charlie cried too.

And another good reason is that Charlie can think of lots of good things to do. Let me tell you about one of them.

Cats like to climb up trees, but they sure hate to climb down. Some cats will sit up in a tree all day and cry until someone comes to help them down. Most people don't help cats in trees. They call the fire department. But my friend Charlie always helps cats.

One day Charlie heard a "miaow" up in a tree. That was the day he invented a new way to get cats out of trees.

He went home and got a bucket and a rope and a fish. He put the fish in the bucket and tied one end of the rope to the handle. He threw the other end of the rope over a limb up above the cat and pulled up the bucket.

2

The cat smelled the fish and jumped into the bucket, and Charlie brought the bucket down.

That cat had an elevator ride and a fish dinner all at the same time. She liked it. Now she won't leave Charlie, follows him everywhere. Charlie says she just wants more fish, but I think she really likes Charlie just as I do.

Janey

BY CHARLOTTE ZOLOTOW

When I walk in the rain
and the leaves are wet
and clinging to the sidewalk
I remember
how we used to walk
home from school
together.

I remember how you had to touch
everything we passed,
the wet leaves

of the privet hedge,
even the stucco part
of the wall.
I only look with my eyes.

I still have the pebble
you found on the playground.
And I remember how
you skipped flat rocks
into the pond.
Mine just sank.

Sometimes when I'm playing
with the other kids
I remember how your voice sounded.
No one else sounds like you.

I remember sometimes
we both talked at once
and when we stopped
we'd said the same thing.
And I remember sitting on the steps

in the sun and not talking
at all.
There is no one else
I can sit with
and not talk.

I remember how
we'd go home for dinner
and I could hardly wait
for dinner to end
to call you.
But sometimes you called me first.

And I remember last Christmas
I half didn't want
to give you your present,
I wanted it so much myself.

You told me later
you half didn't want to give me mine,
but when we each opened our present
it was the *same* book.

I think of you every time
I read the stories over again.

When the wind blows
through the trees at night
I remember how we used to
listen together
nights you slept over.

I didn't want you to move away.
You didn't want to either.
Janey
maybe some day
we'll grow up
and live near each other
again.

I wish you hadn't moved away.

Stevie

BY JOHN STEPTOE

One day my momma told me, "You know you're gonna have a little friend come stay with you."

And I said, "Who is it?"

And she said, "You know my friend Mrs. Mack? Well, she has to work all week and I'm gonna keep her little boy."

I asked, "For how long?"

She said, "He'll stay all week and his mother will come pick him up on Saturdays."

11

The next day the doorbell rang. It was a lady and a kid. He was smaller than me. I ran to my mother. "Is that them?"

They went in the kitchen but I stayed out in the hall to listen.

The little boy's name was Steven but his mother kept calling him Stevie. My name is Robert, but my momma don't call me Robertie.

And so Steve moved in, with his old crybaby self. He always had to have his way. And he was greedy too. Everything he sees he wants. "Could I have somma that? Gimme this." Man!

Since he was littler than me, while I went to school he used to stay home and play with my toys.

I wished his mother would bring somma *his* toys over here to break up.

I used to get so mad at my mother when I came home after school. "Momma, can't you watch him and tell him to leave my stuff alone?"

Then he used to like to get up on my bed

to look out the window and leave his dirty footprints all over my bed. And my momma never said nothin' to him.

And on Saturdays when his mother comes to pick him up, he always tries to act cute just 'cause his mother is there.

He picked up my airplane and I told him not to bother it. He thought I wouldn't say nothin' to him in front of his mother.

I could never go anywhere without my mother sayin'—"Take Stevie with you now."

"But why I gotta take him everywhere I go?" I'd say.

"Now if you were stayin' with someone you wouldn't want them to treat you mean," my mother told me. "Why don't you and Stevie try to play nice?"

Yeah, but I always been nice to him with his old spoiled self. He's always gotta have his way anyway. I had to take him out to play with me and my friends. "Is that your brother, Bobby?" they'd ask me.

"No."

"Is that your cousin?"

"No! He's just my friend and he's stayin' at my house and my mother made me bring him."

"Ha, ha. You gotta baby-sit! Bobby the baby-sitter!"

"Aw, be quiet. Come on, Steve. See! Why you gotta make all my friends laugh for?"

"Ha, ha. Bobby the baby-sitter," my friends said.

"Hey, come on, y'all, let's go play in the park. You comin', Bobby?" one of my friends said.

"Naw, my momma said he can't go in the park cause the last time he went he fell and hurt his knee, with his old stupid self."

And then they left.

"You see? You see! I can't even play with my friends. Man! Come on."

"I'm sorry, Robert. You don't like me, Robert? I'm sorry," Stevie said.

"Aw, be quiet. That's okay," I told him.

One time when my daddy was havin' company I was just sittin' behind the couch just listenin' to them talk and make jokes and drink beer. And I wasn't makin' no noise. They didn't even know I was there!

Then here comes Stevie with his old loud self. Then when my father heard him, he yelled at *me* and told me to go upstairs.

Just 'cause of Stevie.

Sometimes people get on your nerves and they don't mean it or nothin' but they just bother you. Why I gotta put up with him? My momma only had one kid. I used to have a lot of fun before old stupid came to live with us.

One Saturday Steve's mother and father came to my house to pick him up like always. But they said that they were gonna move away and that Stevie wasn't gonna come back anymore.

So then he left. The next mornin' I got up to watch cartoons and I fixed two bowls of corn flakes. Then I just remembered that Stevie wasn't here.

Sometimes we had a lot of fun runnin' in and out of the house. Well, I guess my bed will stay clean from now on. But that wasn't so bad. He couldn't help it 'cause he was stupid.

I remember the time I ate the last piece of cake in the breadbox and blamed it on him.

We used to play Cowboys and Indians on the stoop.

I remember when I was doin' my homework I used to try to teach him what I had learned. He could write his name pretty good for his age.

I remember the time we played boogie man and we hid under the covers with Daddy's flashlight.

And that time we was playin' in the park under the bushes and we found these two dead rats and one was brown and one was black.

And him and me and my friends used to cook mickies or marshmallows in the park.

We used to have some good times together.

I think he liked my momma better than
his own, 'cause he used to call his mother "Mother" and he called my momma
"Mommy."

Aw, no! I let my corn flakes get soggy think-
in' about him.

He was a nice little guy.

He was kinda like a little brother.

Little Stevie.

Boys Just Can't Keep a Secret

BY ASTRID LINDGREN

My name is Lisa, and I am a girl. I have two brothers, who are both older than I am. Karl is eleven years old and Bill is ten. Soon I'll be ten myself, but so far I'm still only nine.

We live on a farm called Middle Farm, because it is between two others. The other two are called North Farm and South Farm. Anna and Britta live at North Farm, and they are girls too. Britta is eleven and—what luck—Anna is just my age.

A boy named Olaf lives at South Farm.

Between his farm and ours is a large linden tree whose branches touch both houses at the upstairs windows. When the boys want to visit each other, they just climb through the tree.

Sometimes we three girls play by ourselves without the boys, and sometimes the boys play without us. But usually we all play together, because most games are more fun when there are six instead of only three.

Every year when it is time to harvest the hay, Daddy says, "This year I don't want any children up in the loft to trample the hay to pieces." But even though he always says this, nobody really believes that he means it.

So all day during the harvest we ride in the hay wagons and jump on the hay in the loft. This year Karl wanted to have a contest to see who dared jump the highest—jump the highest from the top down and not from the bottom up, of course. We climbed up on the beams under the roof and jumped down onto the hay under-

21

neath. My, how it tickled my tummy! Karl had said that the one who won the contest would get a lollipop as a prize. He had bought it that same day at the store in Big Village. We jumped and climbed and climbed and jumped, but finally Karl climbed up as high as he could and leaped down into a tiny little tuft of hay. He landed with a thud and lay still a long time without moving. Later he said he thought that his heart must have fallen down into his tummy and that he would have it in his tummy as long as he lived. Nobody else dared jump from that high, so Karl stuck the prize in his mouth and said, "This lollipop to Karl for brave deeds in the hayloft!"

One day, after Britta and Anna and I had taken a ride in the haywagon with Kalle, the hired man from North Farm, we found a wild strawberry patch behind a pile of stones in a field where we were getting hay. I have never seen so many strawberries! We decided that we should never, never, never tell the boys, or any-

one else, about that strawberry patch. We picked strawberries and strung them on straws, until we had thirteen straws full. In the evening we ate them with sugar and cream. We gave Karl and Bill and Olaf each a couple, but when they wanted to know where we had picked them we said, "We'll never in the world tell you that, because it's a secret."

Then for several days Britta and Anna and I ran around looking for new strawberry patches and didn't bother to play in the hay-loft. But the boys played there. We couldn't understand why they never got tired of it.

One day we said to the boys that now we had seven strawberry patches that we were never going to show them because it was a secret. Then Olaf said, "Haha, that certainly isn't much of a secret compared with ours!"

"What kind of secret do you have?" said Britta.

"Don't tell her, Karl," Olaf said.

But Karl said, "Yes, I will. Then the girls

can hear that our secret isn't as silly as theirs."

"What is it then?" we said.

"We have made nine caves in the hay, if you want to know," Karl said.

"But we won't tell you where," said Bill, and he hopped up and down on one leg.

"We'll soon find them," we said and rushed up into the hayloft to look. We looked all that day and the next, but we didn't find any caves.

The boys thought they were so smart, and Karl said, "You'll never find them. In the first place, you can't find them without a map; and in the second place, you can't find the map."

"What kind of map is it?" we asked.

"A map that we have made," said Karl. "But we have hidden it." Then Britta and Anna and I started to look for the map instead of for the caves. We thought it must be hidden someplace at Middle Farm, because Karl surely would not have let them hide it anywhere else. We looked around in Karl's and Bill's room for hours. We looked in their beds, in their drawers, in their closet, and everywhere.

Finally we said to Karl, "You could at least tell us if it's bird, beast, or fish, the way you do when we play twenty questions."

And then Karl and Bill and Olaf started to laugh, and Karl said, "You may as well give up, because you'll never find the map anyway."

So we didn't look any more. But the next day I was going to ask Olaf if I could borrow *The Arabian Nights* from him, because it was raining and I wanted to stay indoors to read. Karl and Bill were outside, and I went into their room. I was going to climb through the linden tree into Olaf's window.

A little bird had lived in the tree before, and there was a hole in the trunk where he had had his nest. He didn't live there any longer, but when I climbed past his nest I saw a string hanging down from it.

What in the world did the bird use that string for? I thought and pulled the string out.

A roll of paper was tied to the end of the string. It was the map! I was so surprised, I thought I'd fall down out of the tree. I forgot all about *The Arabian Nights* and climbed back into Karl's and Bill's room. I ran over to Britta's and Anna's as fast as I could. I was in such a hurry that I tripped and fell on the stairs and hurt my knee.

My, how happy Britta and Anna were! We hurried to the hayloft with the map, and, before long, we found all the caves. Through the hay the boys had dug long tunnels which were all drawn on the map.

When you creep through one of those tunnels, and it's dark, and there is hay all around, you can't help thinking sometimes: what if I can't get out again? It feels scary and is awfully exciting. But you do always get out.

It was only in the tunnels that it was dark. In the caves it was light, because they were all next to the wall, and light came in through the cracks. They were big, fine caves, and we realized that the boys must have had an awful job

making them. The tunnel to the last cave was so long we thought it would never end. I crept through first, then Britta, and then Anna.

"I bet we've come into a labyrinth that will never end," said Britta.

But just then I saw that it started to get light in front of me, and there was the cave. And—ooh—there sat Karl and Bill and Olaf. You should have seen how surprised they looked when I stuck my nose through the entrance to the cave.

"How did you find your way here?" said Karl.

"Haha, we found the map, of course," I said. "That wasn't very hard."

For a minute Karl was a little put out. But when he had thought a while, he said, "O.K., let's let the girls play too!"

We played all day in the caves, while it rained outside, and had such fun. But the next day Karl said, "Now that you know our secret, you tell us your secret about your strawberry patches. It's only fair."

"That's what you think," we said. "You'll have to find them by yourselves, just as we found your caves."

But to make it a little easier, Britta and Anna and I put arrows made of sticks on the ground. We put the arrows very far apart, though, so it still took the boys a long time to find the strawberry patches. We didn't put down any arrows to show the way to our very best patch. That's our secret, and we are never, never, never going to tell it to anyone.

The Children's Theater

BY CAROLYN HAYWOOD

The very last day of school Eddie arrived with the corners of his mouth turned down and his lower lip sticking out. He looked very unhappy. When Anna Patricia saw him, she said, "Hi, Eddie!"

"Hi!" said Eddie, as he threw himself into his seat and put his head in his hands.

"Don't you feel good?" Anna Patricia asked.

"I feel all right," said Eddie.

"Well, what's the matter with you?" said Anna Patricia.

"Nothing," he replied.

"Oh, that's good," said Anna Patricia. "I'm happy too. I'm happy 'cause I'm going to be an actress."

"Leave me alone," said Eddie. "I don't feel good."

"You just said you felt all right," said Anna Patricia.

"Now I don't," said Eddie.

"Have you got a toothache?" Anna Patricia asked.

"No," said Eddie.

"Headache?" said Anna Patricia.

"No," said Eddie.

"Stomach-ache?" said Anna Patricia.

"No," said Eddie.

Carol, who was standing nearby, pricked up her ears and said, "Are you and Eddie playing a guessing game? Can I play?"

"Oh, go drown yourselves!" said Eddie.

"Eddie Wilson!" exclaimed Anna Patricia. "Here I am trying to help you, and you say, 'Go drown yourself.' I guess you'll be sorry you ever talked to me that way when I'm a real live actress."

Eddie went right on holding his head. Anna Patricia looked at him. Then she said, "Eddie, are you mad at me?"

"No!" said Eddie. "I'm not mad at you. I'm just mad."

"What are you mad about?" said Anna Patricia.

"I'm mad because I can't go to Texas and be a cowboy on my Uncle Ed's ranch," replied Eddie.

"You can't?" said Anna Patricia. "How come?"

"Uncle Ed and Aunt Minnie have to go off on some trip," said Eddie.

"Oh, Eddie! That's too bad. Maybe you could go with us and be an actress," said Anna Patricia.

"What!" Eddie cried, taking his head out of his hands at last.

"I mean an actor," said Anna Patricia.

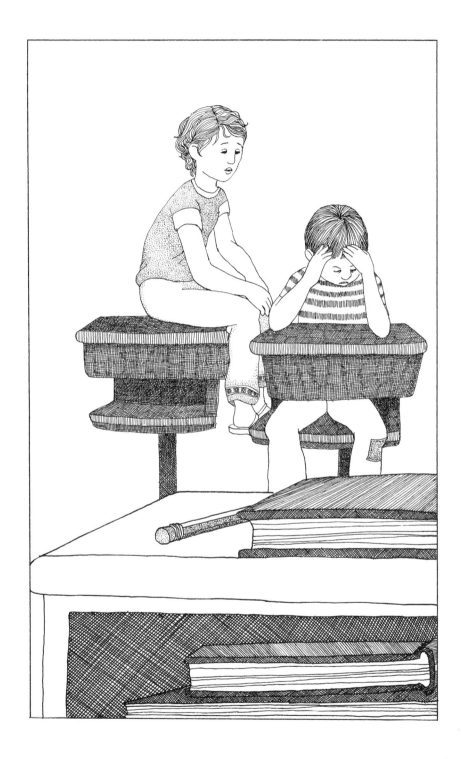

"I don't want to be an actor," said Eddie. "I want to be a cowboy."

"Well," said Anna Patricia, "there are lots of actors on television that are cowboys. Lots!"

That was the last thing that Anna Patricia said to Eddie, because the bell rang for school to begin. When Anna Patricia got home after school, she said to her mother, "Mother, poor Eddie Wilson can't go to Texas and be a cowboy, because his aunt and uncle are going away."

"That's too bad," said her mother. "Is he very disappointed?"

"He feels awful," said Anna Patricia. "I've been thinking. Could he maybe go away with us?"

"Perhaps he could," said her mother. "Of course, there will be your little cousin Davey."

"Davey could sleep in my room," said Anna Patricia.

"Oh, I guess we could manage," said Mrs. Wallace. "Shall I ask his mother if he can go?"

"Yes, ask her," said Anna Patricia.

Mrs. Wallace dialed the Wilson's telephone number. When Mrs. Wilson answered, she said, "This is Mary Wallace. Anna Patricia tells me that Eddie can't go to Texas."

"That's right," said Eddie's mother. "He feels very bad about it, but I've been telling him that something else may come along."

Mrs. Wallace laughed. "Perhaps it has come along," she said. "Anna Patricia and I were wondering whether Eddie would like to spend the summer with us. It isn't like a Texas ranch, but the house is right on the water, and we're getting a sailboat. Then, of course, there is the Children's Theater."

"It sounds wonderful!" said Mrs. Wilson. "How kind of you to invite him. I'll tell Eddie about it."

"We should love to have him," said Mrs. Wallace, before she hung up the receiver.

It wasn't long before Eddie dialed Anna Patricia's telephone number. Anna Patricia answered the ring. "Say, Annie Pat," said Eddie, "it's swell of you to want me to spend the summer with you!"

"Are you coming?" Anna Patricia asked.

"Sure!" said Eddie. "It sounds real keen."

"Mother!" Anna Patricia called out. "Eddie's going with us."

By the first of July, Anna Patricia and her mother, Davey, and Eddie were settled in the house by the water. The front of the house faced the road, but the back porch looked out over the water. At high tide it seemed very near. At first it sounded strange to Anna Patricia to hear the water lapping outside the window of her bedroom, but it wasn't long before she became used to it. Then she didn't notice the sound at all.

Eddie couldn't wait for the sailboat to arrive, and Anna Patricia couldn't wait to see the theater where she was to be an actress.

The very next morning after they arrived, Mrs. Wallace drove the three children over to the theater.

"Annie Pat," said Eddie, when they were seated in the car, "this theater business is your business, but it isn't mine. I'm not going to act."

"Nobody has asked you to act, Eddie," said Anna Patricia.

"Well, they might," said Eddie, "and I haven't time, 'cause I'll be busy with the sailboat as soon as I learn how to sail it."

"Can I go in the boat with you, Eddie?" said Davey.

"You're too little. You might fall overboard."

Davey turned to Anna Patricia. "I was a Wise Man in a play once in kindergarten," he said. "Can I be a Wise Man in a play, Anna Patricia?"

"Wise Men are only at Christmas," said Anna Patricia.

"I was a rabbit, too, once," said Davey.

"Rabbits are only at Easter," said Anna Patricia.

"Well, what *can* I do?"

Before anyone could answer Davey's question, Mrs. Wallace stopped the car beside a large wooden building, and they all got out.

"Is this it?" said Eddie. "This doesn't look like a theater. It's right on the wharf."

"Years ago they built whaling boats in it," said Mrs. Wallace, "but it has been made into a theater."

The children ran to the front door, but Anna Patricia's mother called out, "The front door is locked. Mrs. Wells said we would have to use the back door."

"Oh, yes," said Anna Patricia, "the stage door! Oh, it is so exciting to be an actress!"

"You're not an actress yet," said Eddie.

Around on the side of the building, near the back, they found a door. Eddie turned the doorknob and pushed against the door. As it opened, Mrs. Wallace said, "I'll go do some marketing. I'll come back for you in about an hour."

The sunshine out of doors was so bright

40

that the inside of the building looked very dark. The children could not see very much when they came through the door. But as their eyes became accustomed to less light, they could see that they had come into a very large room filled with rows of benches. It was as large as the assembly room in the children's school.

To the right of the door, there was a stage that filled the back end of the building.

The children could hear a voice on the stage.

"Oh," whispered Anna Patricia, "it's a rehearsal!"

Then a very loud voice said, "Oh, pickles! I love pickles!"

"Let's sit down here and watch it," said Anna Patricia, pushing Davey down into a seat in the front row.

The children looked up at the stage from the front row. There were about ten children sitting on stools. Each one held a paper plate. A boy about Eddie's age was passing a plate of sandwiches.

41

"What kind of sandwiches are these?" asked a little girl.

"Chicken," replied the boy.

"They sure look good," Eddie whispered to Anna Patricia. "They look real."

"They wouldn't have real chicken sandwiches for a rehearsal," said Anna Patricia.

"Maybe they don't eat them," said Eddie.

"I guess not," said Anna Patricia. "Just make believe."

"They've got a lot of stuff up there," said Eddie. "Look at that chocolate cake."

"Looks yummy!" said Anna Patricia.

"When do you suppose they eat all that food?" said Eddie.

"I guess after the play is all over."

"Must be pretty stale!" said Eddie.

Just then Mrs. Wells came in the door. She had a parcel in her arm. "Now," she said, "here is the ice cream, and I don't want it to melt."

"Some play!" said Eddie. "They can't keep ice cream. They're going to eat it, sure enough!"

At that moment Mrs. Wells spied the children in the front row. "Why, Anna Patricia," she called, "I didn't see you there! It's so dark when one comes in out of the sunshine." Mrs. Wells came over to the children and said, "Hello, Davey! How are you?"

"Fine!" said Davey. "I was a Wise Man once, and I was a rabbit."

"Mrs. Wells," said Anna Patricia, "this is Eddie Wilson. He is staying with us this summer."

Mrs. Wells shook hands with Eddie and said, "How nice. I'm glad to see you, Eddie."

Eddie said, "Thanks. I'm glad to meet you."

"Well, isn't this fun!" said Mrs. Wells. "You just came in time. Come right up on the stage."

"Oh, I'm sorry," said Eddie, "but I don't want to act. I really haven't time. I'm going to be awfully busy with the sailboat."

"What is the name of this play that they are rehearsing?" Anna Patricia asked.

44

Mrs. Wells laughed. "This isn't a rehearsal," she said. "This is a picnic lunch. We made so much money at our performance last night that the children are having a feast today. You're just in time."

"Oh!" said Eddie. "Well, that's super!"

Mrs. Wells led the three children through the door that led to the stage. On the stage, she introduced all of the children. "We do this after every play," she said.

"Yes," said a boy named Bruce, "we usually have a supper after the last performance of each play. We call it a Strike Supper."

"Why do you call it a Strike Supper?" Eddie asked.

"'Cause we have to strike down all of the scenery after the last performance," said Bruce.

"Know what, Annie Pat?" said Eddie, sinking his teeth into a chicken sandwich.

"What?" said Anna Patricia, while Eddie chewed a mouthful.

Eddie swallowed and said, "I've changed my mind. I guess I'll be an actor after all."

Two and Me Makes Three

BY ROBERTA GREENE

My name is Joey. I live in a big city called New York. It's bigger than a town, bigger than a village—bigger than almost anyplace. I guess it must be about the biggest place in the whole, wide world—and about the noisiest and the crowdedest, too!

Where I live, the buildings are so close together that there's hardly any room for sky in between. If I want to look at the sky, I really have to look up—straight up!

All kinds of people live on my street—tall

ones and short ones, fat ones and skinny ones. There are children everywhere up and down my street. Two of them I like best of all.

There is my friend Juan. He comes from Puerto Rico. He is just learning how to speak English.

And there is Willie. We're just about the same size, but he sure can play baseball better than I can. He can throw a ball from the little store on the corner all the way up the street to where I live.

We do all kinds of things together, Juan and Willie and me—lots of things. School is a long walk from our street. Every morning we go there together. On the way we watch people hurrying off to work. We see buses pass us covered with signs and splattered with mud, and jammed with people right up to the doors. Busy taxis rush by, squeezing in and out of all sorts of tight places.

There's that big bus up ahead taking people to work. It's jammed full—but look—more

people, and *more people,* and EVEN MORE PEO-
PLE are squeezing inside! I ask Juan and Willie
if they think it will bust.

"Yes," Willie agrees.

"*Si*—I mean yes," says Juan.

Then we have to remind one another to
hurry so we won't be late for school.

We find things to do together before
school, and after school, and, best of all, when
there is *no* school. Sometimes we walk along
and find an empty can that someone has
thrown into the street. Then we see who can
get to it first and who can give it the biggest
kick. Other times we play ball. We take turns
throwing it against the steps and catching it.

You should see us the times when we take
an old broom handle and try to pretend we're
one of the Mets going for another home run.
Boy, wouldn't I like to be a champ like that!

Sometimes we walk through the park. We
whistle, we sing, we play games as we go. It's
fun when Juan walks up in front and Willie and

48

I follow him. If Juan puts up his left hand, so do we. If he walks along the curb, we do, too. We like playing follow-the-leader. Other people in the park think we look pretty silly.

Sometimes they laugh as we parade by—holding our noses and hopping on one foot! But we have too much fun to care. That's what it's like most of the time.

But today is different. This morning I forgot my homework, so Miss Murphy made me stay after school to do it over. I didn't want to stay. I wanted to be outside with Willie and Juan. (Gosh, last night I did everything so quickly. This time I thought I'd *never* get through. I wonder why it took so long.)

Hey! There they are! It sure was nice of them to wait for me.

"Hi, Willie! Hi, Juan! Hey, what's the matter? You fellows look funny. Is anything wrong?"

Juan doesn't answer. He just points to a great big hole in his pants. His mother will be very angry when she sees it. No wonder he doesn't feel like going home yet.

Willie isn't happy either. He ran errands for a long time so that he could buy a birthday present for his mother. Today he was going to buy it, but when he put his hand in his pocket, his money was gone.

He feels awful.

Juan feels awful.

I feel awful, too.

We don't feel like doing much of anything.

What can we do when no one feels happy? We don't want to play ball. We don't feel like singing. We don't want to play kick-the-can or follow-the-leader. We don't want to do anything at all.

No one says a word. We just walk along looking down at the ground. Then all at once I see something round, and scraped, and dirty, with stitches going around it—a real softball— not just a plain old rubber ball like the one Willie has! Who could have left it there? I look

51

all around. I only see a little old lady in a funny gray hat, and another lady pushing a baby carriage. It CAN'T be theirs—so why can't it be M-I-N-E?

"Ouch!"

"Hey, let go! That hurts!"

I don't believe it, but there we are, all three of us in a pile on top of the ball.

"It's mine!"

"I saw it first!"

"You did not!"

And then we start calling one another nasty names and saying terrible things that I'm too ashamed to even think about.

"There it goes!"

"Get it!"

But it's too late. The ball has already rolled off the curb and into the sewer. We just look at one another.

"It's your fault!"

"NO. IT'S YOURS!"

"Why didn't you hang onto it, you—?"

Then we start fighting all over again.

Now I'm alone.

Juan went home by himself.

Willie found a different way home.

I don't have the ball either.

They're not the only kids on the block. Who needs them anyway? I can always find other boys to play with. Why, there's Peter who lives next door, and Ronnie who lives next door to him, and Sammy who lives upstairs from him. It should be easy to find new friends.

I spend a whole week playing with Peter and Ronnie and Sammy and their friends. We're busy all the time. We're all about the same age and we all go to the same school—but somehow things don't feel the same.

Ronnie likes to play ball, but he sure isn't very good at it. He can't throw a ball the way Willie can, and he almost never can catch it. Peter likes to sing, but he never can remember the words to anything. And Sammy likes to play all right, but only if HE'S the leader and if we play what HE wants to play.

I miss my old friends. I wish I'd never seen that silly old ball. I wish that horrible fight had never happened.

Today is Wednesday—a whole week since I've seen Juan and Willie. The other boys stop for me on the way to school. But I don't feel like going with them today.

"You go ahead. I forgot my homework. I'll see you later."

This morning I just want to be by myself. I wish there were some way I could tell Willie and Juan that I'm sorry. I wonder if we'll ever be friends again.

There's Willie standing all alone looking into the window of the corner store.

I'd like to stop and say hello, but I'm too ashamed of myself.

There's Juan on the other corner. He's by himself, too. If only there were some way to make up and be friends again.

We all get to the traffic light at the same time. No one says a word. I wonder if they want to talk to me as much as I want to talk to them. The light changes to red, and we stand there together, but still no one says a word.

There's a big bus up ahead. It's jammed full. Look! More people, and *more people,* and EVEN MORE PEOPLE are squeezing inside!

Without even knowing it, I ask Juan and Willie if they think it will bust.

"Yes," Willie agrees.

"*Si*—I mean yes," says Juan.

"I'M SORRY!" shout the three of us together.

"Come on," says Willie, "or we'll be late for school."

Me and Neesie

BY ELOISE GREENFIELD

It was a good thing for Neesie that Mama couldn't see her, or she would have got a good spanking.

Mama couldn't hear her either, but I could. All the time Mama was cornrowing my hair, Neesie kept calling me and waving her arms around, trying to make me look at her. After a while, I got tired of it.

"Stop it, Neesie!" I said. I couldn't play with her all the time, even if she was my best friend.

Mama pulled my head back around. "Keep your head still, Janell," she said. "And stop talking to yourself."

"I was talking to Neesie, Mama," I said.

"Nobody's in this bedroom but me and you," Mama said. "So if you not talking to me, you talking to yourself."

"Your mother don't know nothing," Neesie said. She made a face at Mama.

I got scared just thinking about Mama seeing her. Sometimes Mama plays games, but she don't never play games like that.

Mama finished my hair and patted it. I could tell I looked pretty by the way she was smiling at me.

She said, "Your father ought to be getting back from the train station with Aunt Bea in a little while. You want to help me fix her lunch?"

"Don't go, Janell," Neesie said. "Let's stay in here and play store."

I didn't know which one I wanted to do. I

said, "Mama, Neesie wants me to play with her."

Mama held her forehead with her hand like she had a headache or something. Then she put her hand on my shoulder and bent down and looked right in my eyes.

"All right, Janell," she said. "But after Aunt Bea gets here, I don't want to hear another word about that Neesie mess. I guess I can stand you making up a friend, but Aunt Bea's old and nervous, and I don't want you upsetting her. You hear me?"

I said, "Neesie's not made up, Mama. She's real!"

"You hear me, Janell?" Mama said.

I told Mama all right, but I wasn't sure I could do it. It was hard not to talk about Neesie when she was always doing things. Right now, she was rolling on the floor and laughing, and I knew she was thinking about Aunt Bea being nervous.

I tried to keep from laughing, but I

couldn't. I put my hand over my mouth and pointed at Neesie. I knew if Mama could see her squinching up her eyes and kicking her skinny legs, she would laugh, too. But Mama just shook her head and went out.

Neesie was laughing so hard, she rolled over on top of my new school shoes.

"Move, Neesie!" I said. "You messing up my school shoes!"

She sat up. I thought she was going to yell back at me like she always does, but she looked like she was going to cry.

I went and sat down beside her.

"What's the matter?" I asked.

"Nothing," she said.

I said, "We going to school tomorrow, re-member?"

Neesie didn't say anything. She had her head down, and I leaned way over so I could see her face better. "Mama said school's going to be fun," I told her.

Then we heard Daddy's voice, and Neesie forgot she was sad. She jumped up and ran

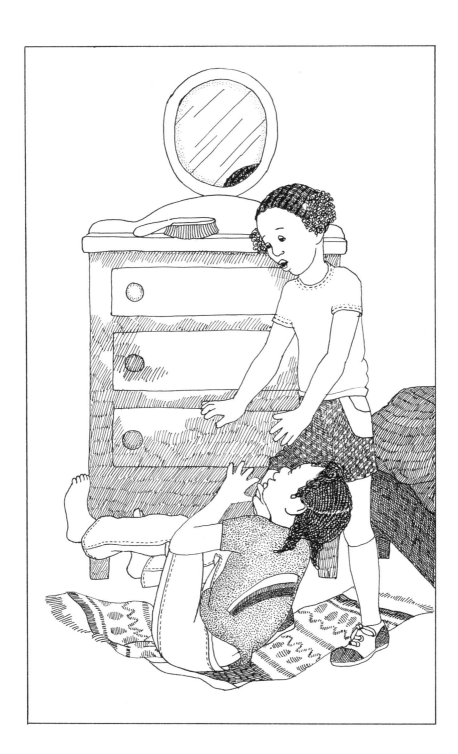

down the hall. I wanted to yell at her to come back, but I remembered what I had promised Mama. So I didn't say anything. I just ran down the hall behind her.

Aunt Bea was standing in front of the sofa, leaning heavy on her walking stick and not letting Daddy and Mama help her. Neesie jumped up on the sofa and sat right behind her.

I said, "Hi, Aunt Bea." But I was looking at Neesie, and Mama was looking at me looking.

"Janell, baby!" Aunt Bea said. "You pretty as ever. Soon as I sit down, I want you to come over here and give me a great big hug."

Neesie was still sitting. She was grinning her bad grin, 'cause she knew I wouldn't let nobody mash her.

I opened my mouth to tell Aunt Bea to move over some, but Daddy reached for her arm.

"Aunt Bea," he said, "why don't you sit over here in this chair?"

"Keep your hands off me, Walter," Aunt Bea said. "Just keep your hands off me. I know where I want to sit and I don't need no help."

I saw her knees bend and her bottom start going down.

"Aunt Bea!" I yelled. "Don't sit on Neesie!"

Aunt Bea said, "Huh? Walter! Is that child seeing ghosts?"

Daddy said, "Take it easy, Aunt Bea, it's just . . . "

But Aunt Bea didn't take it easy. She said, "I'll get it!"

She held onto the arm of the sofa and swung her stick up in the air. She started beating up the sofa.

Neesie was yelling, "Help! Help!" and scooting around to get out of the way. She crawled down to the other end of the sofa, and then she just sat there looking silly like I did one time when I fell down in the store.

"Did I get it, Janell?" Aunt Bea asked. "Did I get it?"

I couldn't talk right then. And Mama couldn't talk either. She was holding her forehead.

But Daddy said, "I think you got it, Aunt Bea."

Neesie slid down off the sofa. "Let's go back in your room, Janell," she said.

I didn't answer her. I didn't want that stick to start flying again. I just said, "I'll be right back, Aunt Bea."

I closed my door so Aunt Bea wouldn't hear me talking. Neesie still had that silly look on her face, and I wanted to laugh, but I didn't want to make her feel bad.

"Aunt Bea's tough, ain't she?" Neesie said.

I said yeah, Aunt Bea sure was tough.

Neesie said, "You can laugh if you want to, Janell. I don't care."

But I wasn't sure.

Then Neesie started laughing, and so did I.

"That's what I get, huh, Janell?" she said. "That's what I get for trying to be so smart."

We put our heads under the pillow so nobody could hear, and we laughed a long time.

But the next morning, Neesie was sad. She wouldn't get up. I wanted to go to school, but she didn't. She kept her head under the covers while Mama helped me get ready.

When me and Mama got outside, I heard Neesie calling me, and I looked up at the window. She was waving, and I waved back.

I didn't think about Neesie too much at school. I had a whole lot of fun with my new friends and my teacher. But when I got home, I wanted to tell Neesie all about it. Only, I couldn't find her. I looked all over and she wasn't there.

I called Mama.

"Shhh," Mama said. "Aunt Bea's trying to sleep."

"Mama," I said, "I can't find Neesie."

Mama said, "You can't?" She looked glad and sorry at the same time. She put her arm around me. "Want me to read you a story?" she said.

I said, "I don't care."

Mama sat in the big chair, and I sat on my little stool and leaned on her lap. She was reading to me, but I wasn't listening. I was thinking about how sad Neesie looked waving to me out the window. And about how she was my best friend and I didn't have nobody to play with before she came.

And then, I got tickled thinking about how silly she looked when she laughed and all the fun we had.

And then, I thought about going to school the next day and playing with my new friends. And I wouldn't never tell them about Neesie. 'Cause she was mine. Just mine.

And then I put my head on Mama's lap, like I always do, and listened to her read.

Tim and Mr. B

BY ELLEN F. BLOOM

Tim walked a block from his new home and stopped to look over a white fence. An old man was sitting in a rocking chair in the yard. He was working away at something on his lap.

"Hello, Mr. Bird," said Tim. "I met you last week with my Mom and Dad."

Mr. Bird looked at him over his glasses. "I remember," he said and went on with his work.

Tim walked on. He isn't very friendly, Tim thought.

Tim's family had just moved from High

Rock to Jefferson. There didn't seem to be any children on their street. Tim hoped he'd find some friends when school started. He really missed Nicky, his best friend in High Rock.

The next time Tim walked past the Birds' house, Mr. Bird was sitting in the same chair working on the same thing. Tim wanted to ask what he was doing, but the old man didn't look up.

A few days later Tim's mother said, "Tim, please take your wagon and go to the store for me. We need bread, milk, and lettuce." Tim bought the groceries at the store, loaded them in his cart and started home.

At the top of a short hill he decided it would be fun to get in the wagon and ride down. It *was* fun! Suddenly, as he neared the street crossing, he saw Mr. Bird carrying a paper bag. Quickly Tim put out his foot, but instead of stopping, the wagon slid sideways and just brushed the old man's leg. Mr. Bird

69

stumbled and down fell his bag, scattering oranges, a can of coffee, and a carton of milk all over the sidewalk.

"Are you hurt? I'm so sorry! It got out of control," Tim burst out, as he hurried to pick up the carton of milk.

"You didn't pay much attention to where you were going, did you?" Mr. Bird said crossly.

Tim felt himself get very red in the face. He didn't look at Mr. Bird as he put the milk, the oranges, and the coffee in his wagon. "I'll pull these home for you," he said.

When they reached Mr. Bird's house, Tim silently handed him the groceries. "I'm sorry," he said again, as he turned to leave.

"Well, no real harm done, son. Nobody got hurt. It's just lucky there weren't any eggs in that bag."

Tim went home wishing Nicky were with him. He remembered how they used to race their wagons down a big hill near his old house, and the many times they had fallen out at the bottom and laughed together.

A few days later he started to the store again. This time Mr. Bird called out to him from the yard.

"Come in," he said.

Shyly Tim pushed open the gate. "I've forgotten your name, son."

"It's Tim."

"Well, Tim, my wife and I thought that if you wanted to make a little money now and then, and it's OK with your Mom and Dad, you could do some shopping for us, too. If I'd give you a list, would you like to do that?"

"Sure!" said Tim, surprised.

When he came back from the store, Mr. Bird was still in the yard. He was holding a piece of wood in one hand and carving it.

"Want to see what I'm doing?"

"Okay." Tim was curious.

"Well, I'm a whittler. I make things out of wood. This is a dog."

"Do you make other kinds of things?" Tim asked.

Mr. Bird smiled a little. "Oh, yes. My Pa taught me when I was about nine and I've been whittling ever since."

The old man sounded a lot more friendly now, and Tim began to forget about the accident. "I'm going to be nine next month." Then, hesitantly, he added, "Could *I* learn?"

"I taught my grandson when he lived here. We did lots of things together. I'd be glad to teach you."

The next morning the phone rang. It was for Tim. "Hello. I have an extra knife I can lend you. Come over and I'll show you how to use it," said a sort of gruff voice.

Tim hurried over and Mr. Bird handed him a piece of soft pine wood. "What would you like to try?"

"An airplane?" Tim asked.

"Whoa there! You have to start on something simpler, like a fish or a bird."

"How about a whale?" Tim asked.

That seemed like a good idea. "Look in this book," said Mr. Bird. "See if you can find a picture of a whale."

"Here's one. He's blue."

"There are two important things you have to know about whittling. You have to have a really sharp knife, and you always work away from you so you don't cut yourself."

Tim took the knife and gave a small push. Nothing happened at all. Mr. Bird put his hand over Tim's and helped guide it so that a big sliver came off. Several times they did this together until Tim began to get the feel. Then he tried it alone.

While he worked, he looked at Mr. Bird's wrinkled hands and the creases in his cheeks and his thin white hair. "How old are you?" he asked.

"Guess," said Mr. Bird.

"Sixty-four?"

"Keep on."

"Sixty-eight?"

"Even more."

"I give up," said Tim.

"Well, it's eighty-six."

"Eighty-six! That's pretty old." Tim looked at him. "Can you run?"

Mr. Bird threw back his head and laughed. "Maybe not as fast as I used to. But, yes, I *can* still run."

Tim went back to his whale. Now he tried to make the head. It was slow work, but he liked the feeling of chipping the wood. He'd have to finish it another time.

Just before he left, Mr. Bird asked, "Hey, have you ever gone fishing?"

"Not really."

"Well, how about coming with me tomorrow?"

At the pond the next day, Mr. Bird put a worm on a hook. He and Tim watched a few fish come and look at it, then swim away. Suddenly one grabbed the worm. Mr. Bird pulled it up on the little dock.

"It looked so dark and round in the water,"

said Tim. "But it's really flat and it has blue and yellow on its sides."

"It's called a sunny. Now you try."

At first Tim had trouble bringing in a fish because he kept jerking the line. Mr. Bird showed him how to keep it slow and steady and Tim finally caught three fish.

While they sat on the dock together Mr. Bird said, "This is like having my grandson. I miss him a lot. You're very good company, just as he was."

As they walked home, Tim said, "I was afraid of you at first. But now, even though you're not my grandfather, I feel as if you are."

"Well, maybe I'm a grand-friend." Mr. Bird laughed. "What would you like to call me?"

Tim thought. "Would Mr. B do?"

"Just fine."

Tim and Mr. Bird shook hands and they walked home without having to talk at all.

The next time Tim went to the Birds', he

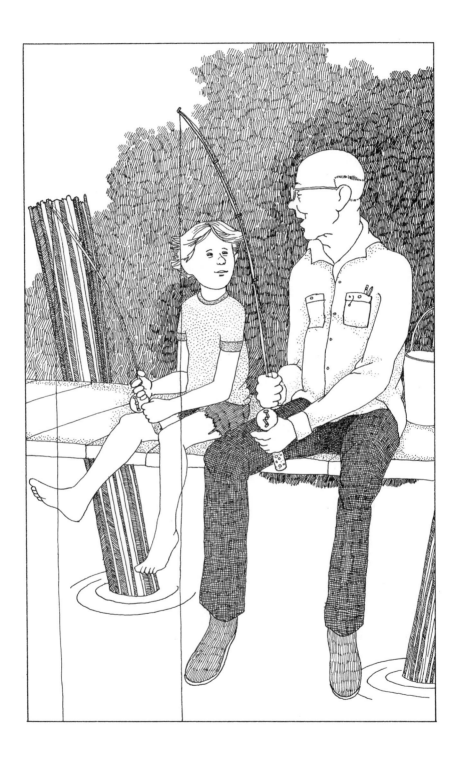

started to dig a blow-hole in his whale's head. Then Mr. B helped him make the eyes.

"Next you can work on the body and the tail. When you have him really smooth with sandpaper, he'll be finished. Then maybe you can try a duck."

During the rest of the summer Tim spent a lot of time with the Birds. Sometimes Tim and Mr. B went for walks in the woods or went fishing. Sometimes Tim worked on his whittling. Sometimes Mr. B was too tired to be with him or he didn't feel good.

Finally the whale was finished and Tim started on the duck. He was so proud of the whale that he had put it on a shelf in his bedroom where it was the first thing he saw every morning.

Then one day Tim had an idea. He took the whale down from its spot on the shelf and ran over to the Birds' house. Mr. Bird let him in and Tim thrust the whale into his hand. "Here," he said quickly. "I want you to have it as a present from me."

Mr. B looked down. "That's one of the nicest things that's ever happened to me," he said. He cleared his throat and his eyes got a little misty. "I'm going to take a nap. When I wake up, I'll see this and think about you."

"That's OK," said Tim, and he ran out of the door and back home.

The next morning the telephone rang early. Father answered. When he hung up he said, "Your mother and I have to go to the Birds'," and they left in a hurry.

When they returned Mother called Tim.

"I know you will be sad," she said. "Your friend Mr. B died last night."

Tim didn't say anything. He couldn't believe it.

Two days later Tim went with his parents to the funeral. Later they all went to the Birds' house. Mrs. Bird took Tim's hand. "Johnny," she said, "this is Tim. He was a very good friend of your grandfather and I want you to meet him. Tim, this is my grandson."

Johnny shook Tim's hand. "My grandfather wrote to me about you and the things you did together."

Later Mrs. Bird gave Tim a hug and said, "Tim, Mr. B said once that he wanted you to have his own whittling knife. Here it is for you to keep."

Tim turned it over and over in his hand. "Thank you," he said quietly.

Later at home Tim went out on the porch holding Mr. B's knife. Father came out a few minutes later and sat beside him.

"Father," said Tim, "I want him to be back."

"I know," said his father.

Tim looked at the knife sadly. "I have to put it away," he said. "If I lose it or break it, I won't have anything to remember him by."

"I think you have a lot to remember him by," said Tim's father.

Tim thought for a moment. "Yes—he taught me to whittle. He taught me to fish."

"So even if you lose his knife, you won't lose what you learned from him. You feel sad,

Tim, but you have a good, good friend to remember."

Tim looked out across the porch toward the Birds' house. He looked down at his knife again. He and his father sat quietly together for several minutes. Finally, Tim stood up and walked slowly to the door. "I think I'll go in and work on my duck for awhile."

Ann Aurelia and Dorothy

BY NATALIE SAVAGE CARLSON

Zing! That's the way it happened. Just like that.

Ann Aurelia Wilson was on the playground all by herself. Of course there were other children there, and a woman was reading a book on the green bench. The boys were playing baseball at one end. That is, they were playing in between the times they were arguing about who was up to bat next or whether somebody was safe or out. Some small children were sitting in the sandbox, building roads or throwing sand.

But Ann Aurelia was all alone, and that's the way it had been most of the summer. She pumped higher and higher in the swing, with her head back so the wind could blow across her face and ruffle her short-cropped hair. Her legs, covered by worn denim slacks, were thrust straight out. Her sweat shirt hung shapelessly.

Ann Aurelia didn't see the little girl taking a shortcut past the swing. She was a spindly little girl with hair in two exact braids and horn-rimmed glasses that had slipped halfway down her nose.

Just as the girl crossed in front of the swing —*zing*—the chain broke and Ann Aurelia thumped into her. Both girls sprawled in the scrabbled dirt.

"Oops!" exclaimed Ann Aurelia. "Sorry! Did I hurt you?"

The girl picked up herself and her glasses. "Nope. Didn't break my glasses either. I busted them twice already."

"And I sure busted the swing," said Ann Aurelia.

Both girls dusted themselves off, and Ann Aurelia straightened the stiffly starched bow in back of the other girl's blue gingham dress.

"What's your name?" she asked.

"Dorothy."

"Dottie?"

"Just plain Dorothy. That's what everybody calls me. What's yours?"

"Ann Aurelia."

"Both?"

"Yep."

"Not Ann or Aurelia?"

Ann Aurelia shook her head. "I was named after two grandmas who didn't like each other. So they couldn't call me just Ann or just Aurelia because the other would get mad."

"I knew you were a girl all the time. You live near here?"

"Down that street. I live with Mrs. Hicken now. First I lived with Mrs. Jolly. She's the one

83

got my hair cut short so it wouldn't be so much trouble to wash and comb. I like it this way. Sometimes I can play with boys a long time before they find out I'm a girl."

"Why did you leave Mrs. Jolly? She sounds like fun—her name, I mean."

"Her married daughter moved in with her children. So the agency put me with Mrs. Swann. Her husband was nice. He used to give me money for candy, but Mrs. Swann would make me hand it over to her because he never gave her half enough to buy the groceries."

"Where's your real honest mother?"

Ann Aurelia's face hardened and tightened. "Out west. But she's not caring where I am, so I'm not caring where she is."

Dorothy realized that she had touched a sore subject. "You like this Mrs. Hicken? Is she nice to you?"

"She's the best. She lets me eat sandwiches in bed. She even lets me make them myself— out of whatever's in the refrig. Last night I had a baloney on rye with some hot peppers and

84

peanut butter and strawberry jam that was left over." She paused dramatically. "And then I gooped whipped cream all over it and ate it with a spoon."

Dorothy's eyes behind her thick glasses grew even bigger with admiration. "I sure can see that sandwich even without these glasses."

"Let me have a look through them," said Ann Aurelia, stretching out her hand. Dorothy obligingly pulled off her glasses and handed them over.

Ann Aurelia put them on with a flourish. *"Zowie!* Everything looks big and blurred."

"I started out with them in first grade. Before that I thought everybody had nothing in back of them."

Ann Aurelia took a few hesitant steps over the crab grass, her hands held out as if she were walking a tightrope. Then she primly folded her arms and lifted her freckled nose into the air. "I'm Miss Watson from the agency now." She spoke in a voice as deep as she could drop it. " 'Mrs. Hicken, you may find Ann Aurelia a

85

spirited child but she *can* be controlled.' I heard her say that when I was listening from the kitchen."

Dorothy fizzed with giggles. "You sure are a case. I think you're just the most fun. But you better give me back my glasses. Mama said she'd blister me if I broke them again."

"Mothers!" scoffed Ann Aurelia, returning the glasses. "Who needs them?"

"I'm used to mine so I wouldn't want to keep changing from a Mrs. Cut-off-your-hair to a Mrs. Hicken-Chicken."

Ann Aurelia shook with an exaggerated mirth. "Dorothy, you're just the funniest yourself. When you came by, something went *zing* inside me."

"Me too."

"Bet we can have a lot of fun together."

"Sure will."

"What shall we do first?" asked Ann Aurelia.

"Maybe we can fix this old swing and pump up together."

"Okay. But the link's rusted through."

"If we could find a piece of rope or wire—"

"If there was anything like that loose around here, the boys would have gone off with it," reasoned Ann Aurelia.

"I've got a big idea," said Dorothy. "What about using my handkerchief? It won't get dirty, will it? Because my Aunt May gave it to me on my birthday."

"I'll rub off the links first with my sweat shirt. It's got to go into the wash sometime."

Ann Aurelia stretched the bottom of the shirt and stooped to rub the links with it. Then Dorothy pulled her handkerchief into sharp points and threaded them through.

"I'll tie the knot," offered Ann Aurelia. "There was a Boy Scout lived next door to the Swanns, and he showed me how to tie a knot so it won't come loose. He wanted me to join the Scouts too, at first."

She deftly made the knot. Then she cautiously took hold of the chains and stepped up on the board seat.

"It's holding, Dorothy. I knew it would. You get on too, and see if it'll hold both of us."

"Okay, A.O."

"A.O.?"

"For Ann Aurelia. It's faster that way."

"Aurelia doesn't begin with *o*. It's *A-u-r-e-l-i-a*."

"Okay, A.A. It's a jawbreaker no matter how you spell it."

"My Grandma Wilson must have been named after somebody else too. Now let's shut up and save our breath to pump."

The children squatted and stretched themselves in turn as they pulled against the chains with their hands and pushed against the board with their feet. Higher and higher into the air they went. Dorothy's blue skirt ballooned in the wind and Ann Aurelia's slacks tightened over her knees.

"We've sure got her going," panted Ann Aurelia. "Bet riding in an airplane is just like this."

"Maybe we can make us go all the way over," gasped Dorothy. "I saw a man in the circus do it one time."

"We'll loop-the-loop."

Perhaps the swing would have looped-the-loop if it had been in good condition. The knot in the handkerchief still held, but there was an agonizing *ri-i-ip!* The board swung loose at one end. Dorothy flapped into the air like a young bluebird learning to fly. Ann Aurelia clung desperately to one chain like a mountain climber on a rope.

The woman on the green bench screamed and threw her book into the air. The boys stopped playing ball and came running over. Some people no one had seen before appeared as if by magic.

Dorothy lay in the sparse grass. She lay very still with one arm and one leg thrown out like a doll that is tired of being played with.

Ann Aurelia brought the swinging chain to a halt and jumped from it. She ran to Dorothy and dropped on her knees. She shook her frantically.

"Wake up, Dorothy!" she begged. "Please wake up! We don't have to play on the swing anyhow. Let's go down the slide."

Sharp fingers dug into Ann Aurelia's shoulders. They pulled her to her feet.

"Never touch anyone who's been injured," scolded the woman who had been sitting on the bench. "You might make things worse."

"They're calling the ambulance," announced a man in a straw hat. "Everybody stand back so she can get air. Stand back, sonny," he ordered Ann Aurelia.

"Who is she?" the woman asked Ann Aurelia. "What's her name?"

"Dorothy."

"Dorothy who?"

"I don't know. Just plain Dorothy."

"Where does she live?"

"Don't know that either. She never said. I didn't even think to ask her."

They heard the screeching of the siren before they saw the white ambulance. It swerved around the corner, its red dome-light flashing like a firecracker about to go off. It pulled up to the curb. Two men in white jackets jumped out. They opened the doors in back and quickly brought out a stretcher.

"Stand back, everybody," ordered one of the men. "Make way."

Ann Aurelia stepped farther back. She stood watching the men ease Dorothy onto the stretcher. She watched them carry her to the ambulance. Then the doors closed and one of the men got in front. The ambulance shot away. Ann Aurelia could hear its long drawn-out siren fading into the distance—like a yelping dog beaten in a fight.

Ann Aurelia bowed her head in loneliness. Then she saw the horn-rimmed glasses lying in the grass. She picked them up. Broken glass fell out of one side. The other was neatly cracked.

Ann Aurelia sat down in the grass with her

knees drawn up and her head between them. She sniffled a few times, then wiped her nose on a slack leg.

"What's the matter?" asked the woman, who had returned to the bench and was trying to find her place in the book. "Were you hurt too?"

Ann Aurelia shook her head between her knees. "They're all gone," she said, her voice muffled by the slacks. "And now Dorothy's gone too."

She pressed the broken glasses tightly against her sweat shirt.

Mrs. Hicken was a comfortable-looking woman. You knew that she liked spaghetti and pastry just by looking at her. She was sitting in a big overstuffed chair that matched her when Ann Aurelia came in the door with a loaf of bread in her hands.

"It's come!" shouted Ann Aurelia, looking at the newspaper that Mrs. Hicken was reading. "I've been waiting for it, and now it has to

come just when I've gone after the bread."

"What's come, dearie?"

"The paper," cried Ann Aurelia. She was itching to grab it from Mrs. Hicken's hands, but that wouldn't be polite. "Does it say anything about a little girl named Dorothy getting killed on the playground—or hurt?"

"A friend of yours? I noticed you've been in the dumps since yesterday."

"She was for a little while until the swing broke."

Mrs. Hicken was not one to give up her newspaper, especially when she was so comfortably seated for reading it.

"Old Mrs. Hentzler died, but her time had come. She's the mother of Fred Hentzler, runs the bakery. Must have been hard for her to leave all those pies and chocolate eclairs."

"But Dorothy! Doesn't it say anything about her?"

Mrs. Hicken rustled the paper. "I'll look in the accident column. Here we are!

"This must be her."

94

DOROTHY GRANT, AGED TEN, OF 62 WEST STREET, WAS TAKEN TO THE HOSPITAL AT 3:30 P.M. YESTERDAY AFTER A FALL FROM A SWING ON THE PLAYGROUND. SHE WAS TREATED FOR A BUMP ON THE HEAD AND RELEASED.

Ann Aurelia was overcome with joy. "She's alive and she's all right. And West Street isn't far from here. Can I go to see her right now, Mrs. Hicken? I have to give her back her glasses."

"No reason you can't, dearie, but be sure to get home by four o'clock. I've got to take you to the dentist. Miss Watson is real strict about such things."

"I'll be back," cried Ann Aurelia, throwing the loaf of bread onto a chair before she raced out the door.

She began racing down the street, but slowed to a walk when she ran out of breath.

The houses crowded closer together and drew nearer to the sidewalk as Ann Aurelia approached West Street. She quickened her steps again. It wasn't far to Number 62 now. It was a neat one-story house with a hydrangea bush filling the tiny square of yard.

Ann Aurelia hurried up the steps and knocked on the door. A slender woman, with straight black hair drawn into a bun high on her head, answered.

"Does Dorothy live here?" asked Ann Aurelia breathlessly.

"Come in, little boy," invited the woman, opening the screen door. "She's sweeping her room now."

"I'm a girl."

"That's all right. You can come in anyway."

Dorothy appeared from the shadowed inner door. There was a big white bandage on her forehead. She squinted at Ann Aurelia; then she went closer and stared in her face.

"It's A.A.," she cried happily. "Thought maybe you were somewhere in the hospital too. We sure had us a swinging."

"I'm okay. Mrs. Jolly used to say I had a charmed life—seeing all the things that happened to me. I brought your glasses back." She pulled them out of her pocket. "But they're busted worse than the swing."

"Thank goodness," said Dorothy's mother. "I looked all over the playground for them before dinner last night. I'll take them straight down to the optometrist. Dorothy can't half see without them. You stay and play with her. She'll have to watch Louise while I'm gone."

For the first time, Ann Aurelia noticed the little girl standing near Dorothy. She was a plump child, with her little round stomach pushing her belt up and a finger in her mouth.

"She's my little sister," explained Dorothy. "Take your finger out of your mouth, Louise, and say 'howdy' to my friend."

Louise took the finger from her mouth long enough to repeat "howdy," then put it back again.

"I won't be gone too long unless there are

some ahead of me," said Mrs. Grant. "Dorothy, you make up some fruitade for—what's your name, little girl?"

"Ann Aurelia, after my grandmas."

"Ann Aurelia who?"

"Wilson. That was my father's name when he was alive."

"Well, fix some fruitade for all of you, Dorothy. Don't spill any on the kitchen floor. I just washed it this morning. And clean up after you."

She put the glasses in her handbag and went out the door. Ann Aurelia and Dorothy stood staring at one another.

"Does it hurt under the bandage?" asked Ann Aurelia.

"Nope, but there's a bump big as a walnut. See!" She pulled off the bandage. "I don't really have to keep it on, but it makes everybody treat me nicer."

Ann Aurelia was impressed. "You've sure got a good one. It's as big as the one I got the time I fell off Mrs. Jolly's roof. But I didn't get to ride in an ambulance like you did. Oh, I was bandaged and home before I knew what happened. Mr. Jolly brought home a gallon of ice cream, and he let me eat all I wanted."

Dorothy slipped the bandage back in place. "And maybe Daddy will bring me some ice cream."

"I thought I'd lost you for good," said Ann Aurelia. "I don't have any other friends. It's hard to make friends when you move to a new place in the summer. I used to live on the other side of town."

"I guess it must be. I've lived right here all my life."

"We'll probably go to the same school."

"Sure will. It's Jefferson."

"I'll be in fifth grade."

"Me too. We'll be in Miss Bennett's room. Everybody's crazy about her. She's so nice and pretty. Last year I had Miss Wyckoff. *Glap!* She's almost a hundred years old. Even Hughie went to school to her. He always said she's a nightmare."

"Who's Hughie?"

Dorothy pointed to the photograph on the mantelpiece. It was of a young man in Navy uniform. "He's my brother. He's off on the west coast now. Sure looks swell in his uniform. Even the girls who didn't use to like him go for him now when he's home."

"You're lucky with a big brother and little sister. There was a boy put out with Mrs. Jolly, too, but he wasn't my brother."

"I've got a big sister too. Shirley. She works in the five-and-ten and pays board to Mama and Daddy. She always gives me a quarter on payday. Let's get busy with the fruitade. Good thing I don't need glasses for the directions. I've made it so much all summer."

Ann Aurelia followed Dorothy into the small kitchen, and Louise tagged along. Ann Aurelia's sharp eyes took in the gas stove which, although very old, was clean and tidy.

Not like Mrs. Hicken's with blobs of grease blackened on the burners and dark places in the grooves of the knobs. Or like Mrs. Swann's kitchen that was so clean you couldn't even make a sandwich unless you washed the butter knife before you ate the sandwich. It was more like Mum's kitchen, with the pot of something that smelled so good simmering on the back burner, and the matching dish towels with little cutouts of radishes and carrots sewed in the corners.

Dorothy set the broom in the corner and went to the refrigerator.

"You get the fruitade," she ordered Ann Aurelia. "It's on the bottom shelf there with the dry soups. Take whatever flavor you want."

While Dorothy pulled out the ice tray and pinched out the cubes, Ann Aurelia looked through the colored packets. "Let's try cherry. I like cherries. One time I ate a whole big bag of them by myself. Boy, was I ever sick! I swallowed most of the pits too."

"A.A., I'm thinking we don't want plain fruitade. Let's make something special like you did with the sandwich."

"Suits me. What have you got in the refrig besides that ice?"

Dorothy swung the door open again. "What's that bottle? I can't see without my glasses."

"It's catsup."

"I never had a drink with catsup in it, did you?"

"I've had tomato juice but it wasn't in any cherry drink," admitted Ann Aurelia.

"Let's try it. Not too much though."

"Here! I'll just drop in a blob. Oops! That's more than I meant. I think we got too much."

"Then we ought to put something else in to kill the taste," suggested Dorothy. "I know that's apple butter in this jar."

"Looks like it. That ought to thicken it some. Where's a spoon?"

"In that top drawer."

Ann Aurelia spooned apple butter into the pitcher while Dorothy stirred vigorously.

"It doesn't mix right," complained Ann Aurelia.

"Maybe we could use the eggbeater on it," said Dorothy.

She fumbled for the eggbeater in the lower drawer. She whipped the drink into a froth.

"Mrs. Swann used to beat an egg into milk that way every morning for Mr. Swann," said Ann Aurelia. "He liked eggnog."

"Why don't we whip up an egg in this as long as we've got to wash the eggbeater anyhow?"

"Why not? If it was good enough for Mr. Swann, it ought to be good enough for us. He was real finicky."

Dorothy cracked the egg on the rim of the pitcher. "Oh, oh! Some of the shell went in too."

"That won't matter."

Dorothy frowned. "It looks muddy.

Maybe it's because I don't have my glasses."

"It's no particular color at all."

"Mama has some food coloring in the closet. Why don't you pick out a color you like?"

Ann Aurelia examined the little bottles. "There's red and yellow and blue and—"

Louise spoke for the first time. "I like blue."

"I never did drink anything blue," confessed Ann Aurelia, "not even medicine. Let's make it blue like Louise wants."

Dorothy churned the eggbeater awhile longer. "It's still a funny color."

"We don't care. We better put a lot of sugar in it to sweeten up all that egg and catsup."

"There's maple syrup in the cupboard. It's even better than sugar."

After the syrup was added, both girls studied the pitcher thoughtfully.

"It looks awful," said Ann Aurelia.

"We'll try it on Louise first," decided Dorothy. "You want some of this yummy, scrumptious, special drink, Louise?"

The little girl took her finger from her mouth and nodded eagerly.

Dorothy selected a glass from the cupboard and poured it full of the mixture. She handed it to her sister. She and Ann Aurelia stood staring intently at the child as she slowly downed the drink. When it was gone, Louise looked into the empty glass. Then she held it out.

"More," she ordered.

The older girls were delighted.

"We've invented a new drink." Dorothy began a jerky little dance between the sink and the refrigerator. *"A-poof! E-poof! I-poof!"* she chanted.

Ann Aurelia joined her, hopping stiffly from one foot to the other. *"O-poof! U- and Y-poof!* We've poofed a brand new drink nobody's ever had before."

"Nobody but Louise. Let's poof some of it into glasses for us."

She did so after refilling Louise's glass. "We'll poof us a party."

Each girl took a slow sip.

"It tastes funny," said Dorothy, "but it's sweet enough."

"Anything this sweet ought to be good."

They slowly drained their glasses.

"Want more?" asked Dorothy.

"It's pretty rich. Maybe we ought to wait awhile."

"Better we let it settle and do something else before we drink more. You want to peek into Shirley's room and see all her stuff? She's got the most clothes. Sometimes I try them on when she's gone."

Ann Aurelia followed Dorothy into a tiny pink bedroom. The skirted dressing table and a bed covered with a rose print almost filled it. Ann Aurelia was most interested in the dressing table.

"Mum had one just like this. And she had about a hundred kinds of lipsticks."

107

"So has Shirley, and a lot of other gook too. What did your mum look like?"

Ann Aurelia hesitated a moment, then she said, "She had eyes like violets and lips like a rosebud and—and—she walked with a regal air."

Dorothy stared. "You don't say! Shirley doesn't look anything like that, but she's real pretty. Oh, we better get out of here! I hear Mama coming in the front door. I'll show you Shirley's clothes some other time. We can both try them on."

"*Oops!* I bet it's late. I've got to get myself home. Have to see the dentist at four."

"I'll walk a way with you."

"Will you? That'll make it go faster."

Mrs. Grant smiled at them. "Did you children have a good time? Did you have enough fruitade?"

"Yes," answered Dorothy. "We made more than enough. Maybe Louise can finish it off. She likes blue."

"Did you clean up your mess?"

Dorothy's look of surprise was mixed with shame. "We forgot."

"We'll do it right away," offered Ann Aurelia. "I'm in no hurry to get to the dentist."

Mrs. Grant sighed. "Run along, both of you. I'll do it myself. But remember what I'm always telling you, Dorothy. This is positively the last time."

"I'll wash the dinner dishes tonight," said Dorothy. "I'll even scrape them. And you better eat everything on your plate, Louise, or we'll never make you a special drink again."

The girls walked up the street arm-in-arm.

I Need a Friend

BY SHERRY KAFKA

All by myself
I can dig for treasure
But I need a friend
to hold the map.

All by myself
I can grow a flower
But I need a friend
to give it to.

All by myself
I can throw a ball
But I need a friend
to catch it.

All by myself
I can tell a joke
But I need a friend
to laugh.

All by myself
I can climb a tree
But I need a friend
to give me a boost.

All by myself
I can draw a picture
But I need a friend
to look at it.

All by myself
I can eat a sandwich
But I need a friend
to have a picnic.

All by myself
I can run
But I need a friend
to race.

All by myself
I can skin my knee
But I need a friend
to feel sorry.

All by myself
I can know a secret
But I need a friend
to whisper it to.

112

All by myself
I can guess a riddle
But I need a friend
to tell it.

All by myself
I can dream a story
But I need a friend
to listen to it.

All by myself
I can play alone
But I need a friend
for sharing.